Have a
great
Summer!
♥
Joey

To Karina, Karla, Mahvash, and Marisa,
who also share memories of fairy tales —S.E.

To Jake, Justin, and the one on the way; to Kimpy,
Toughie, Fifi, Mr. Bluebird, and a hot latte —M.M.

Text copyright © 2005 by Susan Middleton Elya
Illustrations copyright © 2005 by Mercedes McDonald

Typeset in Dolores. Designed by Steffanie Levin
Illustrations created with pastels

Published by Bloomsbury Publishing, New York and London

Library of Congress Cataloging-in-Publication Data
Elya, Susan Middleton.
Fairy trails / Susan Elya ; illustrated by Mercedes McDonald.
p. cm.
Spanish words and phrases used throughout English text.
Summary: Miguel and Maria meet various fairy tale characters as they walk
to their aunt's house. Includes some Spanish words.
ISBN-10: 1-58234-927-4 (alk. paper)
ISBN-13: 978-1-58234-927-5
[1. Characters in literature—Fiction. 2. Stories in rhyme] I. McDonald, Mercedes, ill. II. Title.
PZ8.3.E514Fai 2004   [E]—dc22   2003062943

First U.S. Edition 2005
Printed in China
3 5 7 9 10 8 6 4 2

Bloomsbury Publishing, Children's Books, U.S.A.
175 Fifth Avenue
New York, NY 10010

Glossary

abuela (ah-BWEH-lah) grandma

alfombra (ahl-FOME-brah) rug, carpet

amigos (ah-MEE-goce) friends

beso (BEH-soe) kiss

brujita (broo-HEE-tah) little witch

canela (kah-NEH-lah) cinnamon

casita (kah-SEE-tah) cottage

día (DEE-ah) day

el grande (EHL GRAHN-deh) the big one

fina (FEE-nah) fine

hada madrina (AH-dah mah-DREE-nah) fairy godmother

hola (OE-lah) hello

huevo (WEH-voe) egg

la derecha (LAH deh-REH-chah) the right

la izquierda (LAH eez-KYEHR-dah) the left

lobo (LOE-boe) wolf

mamá (mah-MAH) mom

mañana (mah-NYAH-nah) tomorrow

manzanas venenosas (mahn-SAH-nahs veh-neh-NOE-sahs) poisonous apples

mediana (meh-DYAH-nah) middle one

osos (OE-soce) bears

papá (pah-PAH) dad

peligro (peh-LEE-groe) danger

pequeño (peh-KEH-nyoe) small one

puerta (PWEHR-tah) door

rosas (RROE-sahs) roses

¿Qué tal? (KEH TAHL) How's it going?

quesadillas (keh-sah-DEE-yahs) cheese and tortilla sandwiches

queso (KEH-soe) cheese

tía (TEE-ah) aunt

tortillas (tohr-TEE-yahs) flat, thin bread made from cornmeal or flour

vecinos (veh-SEE-noce) neighbors

vía (VEE-ah) way, path

zapatilla de cristal (sah-pah-TEE-yah DEH krees-TAHL) glass slipper

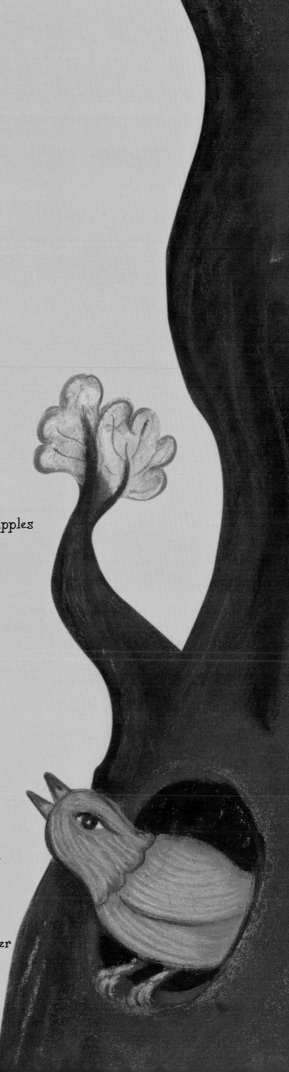

Miguel and María, on one summer **día**,
left home to go visit their auntie—their **tía**.

At the crossroads, Miguel asked her, "Which way to go?
To the right—**la derecha**?"
María said, "No. Go to the left—**la izquierda**—instead."
But Miguel was too slow, so she went on ahead.

"I will follow *the* **vía** *to* find my María,
then hurry *to* Auntie's *for* hot **quesadillas**."
But now—so confusing—which path should he follow?
That cottage seemed strange in *the* woods *by the* hollow.

But María had entered the candy **casita**
with a tiny old woman, a witch—a **brujita**.
Miguel was so worried he circled round back
to enter the cottage and plan his attack.

The witch couldn't see much but wanted her dinner.
María was clever and acted much thinner,
then said, "I must go now and take to my **tía**
this cheese—tasty **queso**—to melt in **tortillas**."

Outside was a **lobo**, a wolf with long tail.
He said, "Hey, **amigos**, you're using my trail.
Do I smell a pastry with cinnamon—**canela**?
Right there in your basket, for Grandma—**Abuela**?"
Miguel tapped María, said,
"Don't talk to strangers.
A hungry old wolf spells **peligro**,
real danger!"

They ran through the trees
till they came to a glen
where they met a young lady
and seven small men.
They said to the maiden,
with skin soft as **rosas**,
"Beware poisoned apples—
manzanas venenosas!"

Then they passed by a
pumpkin hitched up to six mice.
On top sat a housemaid—
they had to look twice.
That gal wasn't shy. She said, "**Hola. ¿Qué tal?**"
She held a glass slipper—**zapatilla de cristal**.
"Have you seen Fairy Godmother, **Hada Madrina**?
I just want to tell her last night was so **fina**."

The pair hurried on, saw *three* bears on a walk,
and Miguel and María heard each of them talk.
The big one, **el grande**, and *the* middle, **mediana**,
said, "Come along, Baby! Today! Not **mañana**!"

Said *the* small one—**pequeño**—"I'm hungry, **Papá**.
You *think* *that* our porridge has cooled yet, **Mamá**?"
Miguel asked *the* bears, "Is your **puerta** locked tight?
You might want *to* check, see if things are all right."

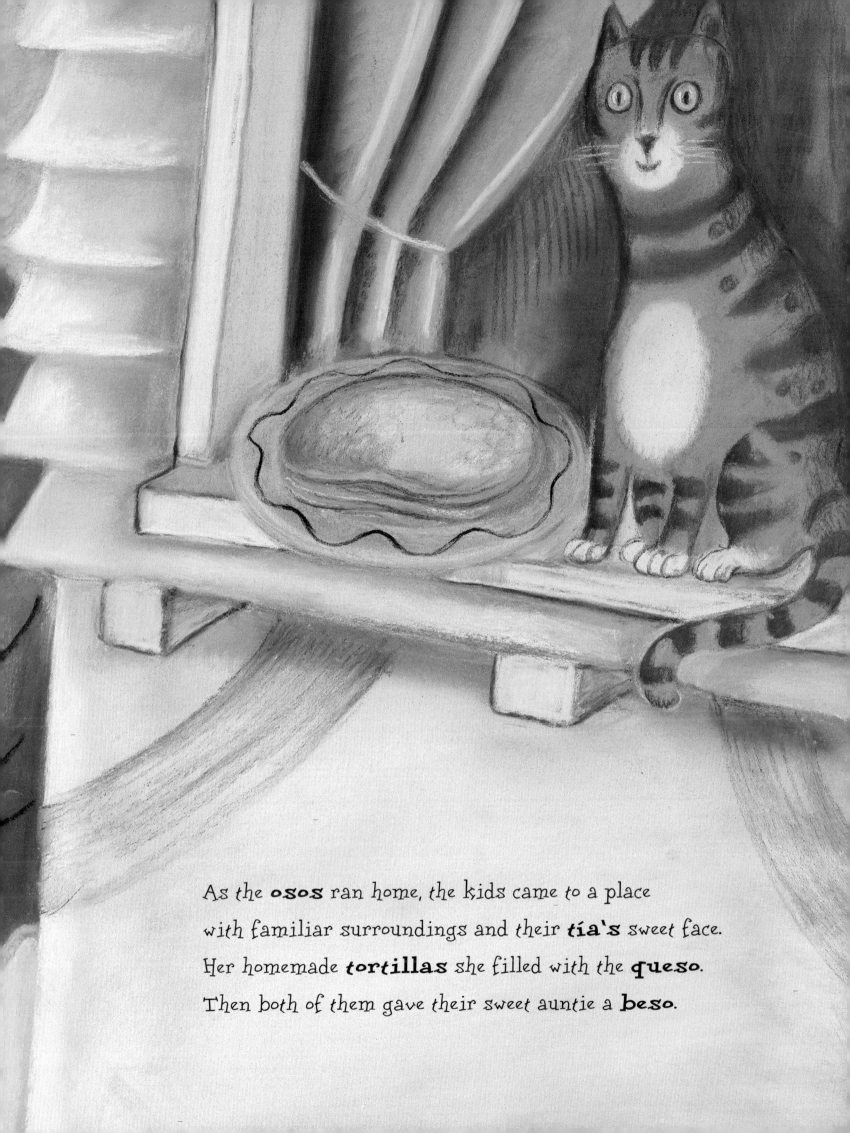

As the **osos** ran home, the kids came to a place
with familiar surroundings and their **tía's** sweet face.
Her homemade **tortillas** she filled with the **queso**.
Then both of them gave their sweet auntie a **beso**.

Miguel and María, on *their* last **quesadilla**,
said, "Auntie, your neighbors? It's been a strange **día**."
"My **vecinos**?" she asked. "They're a good bunch of folk.
Except Humpty **Huevo**. He's a really bad yolk."

Then Miguel and María walked home through the trees
with their now-empty basket (they'd used up the cheese).
They came to a fork—to the left or the right?
If they went the wrong way, then they'd be there all night!

So they asked a nice boy
with a rug by his side,
"Your magic **alfombra**,
will it give us a ride?"